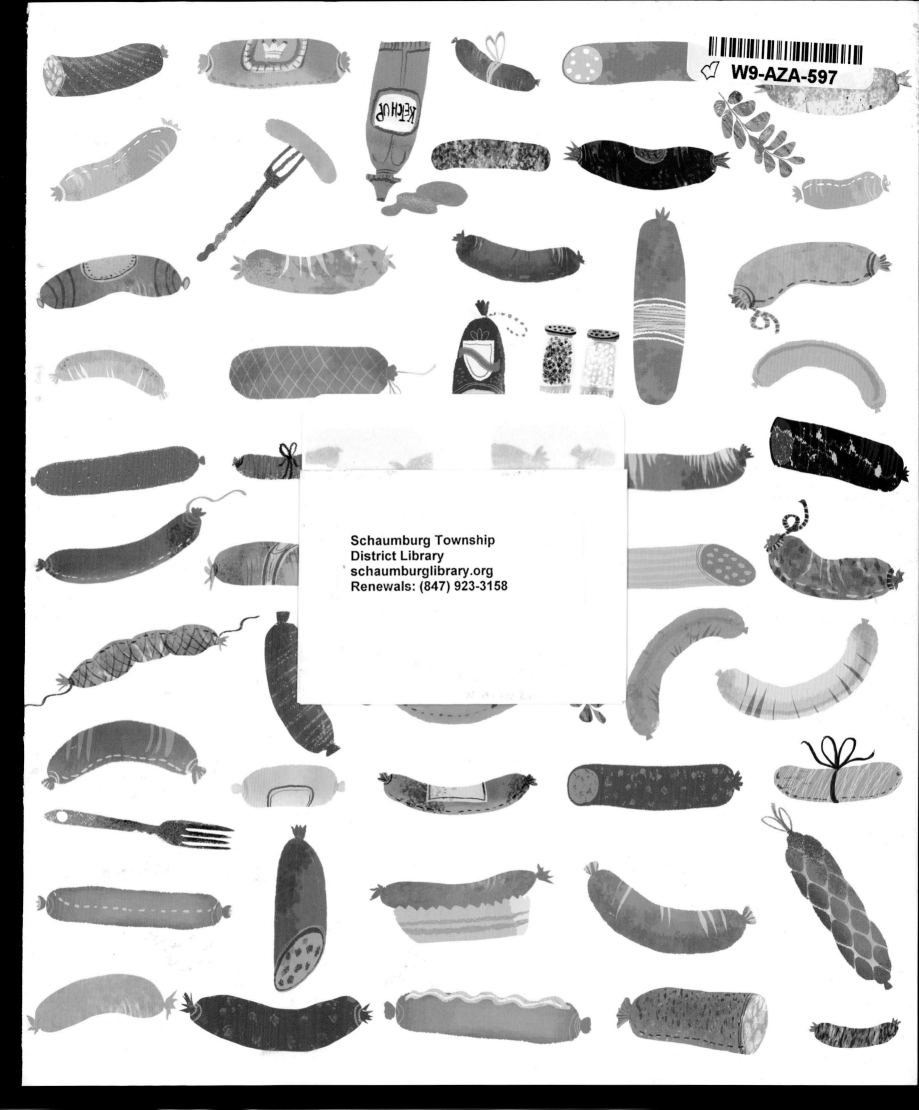

To my niece Sheri
and her ginger cat

First U.S. edition 2017

Library of Congress Catalog Card Number pending
ISBN 978-0-7636-9297-1

17 18 19 20 21 22 TLF 10 9 8 7 6 5 4 3 2 1

Printed in Dongguan, Guangdong, China

This book was typeset in Adobe Caslon Pro.
The illustrations were created digitally.

TEMPLAR BOOKS

an imprint of
Candlewick Press
99 Dover Street
Somerville, Massachusetts 02144
www.candlewick.com

One Hundred Sausages

Yuval Zommer

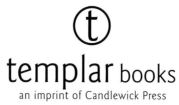

templar books

an imprint of Candlewick Press

Scruff's favorite things in the
whole wide world were
SAUSAGES!
Especially the ones in the
butcher's window.

Wherever Scruff went (and he went everywhere),

he always sniffed out the sausages.

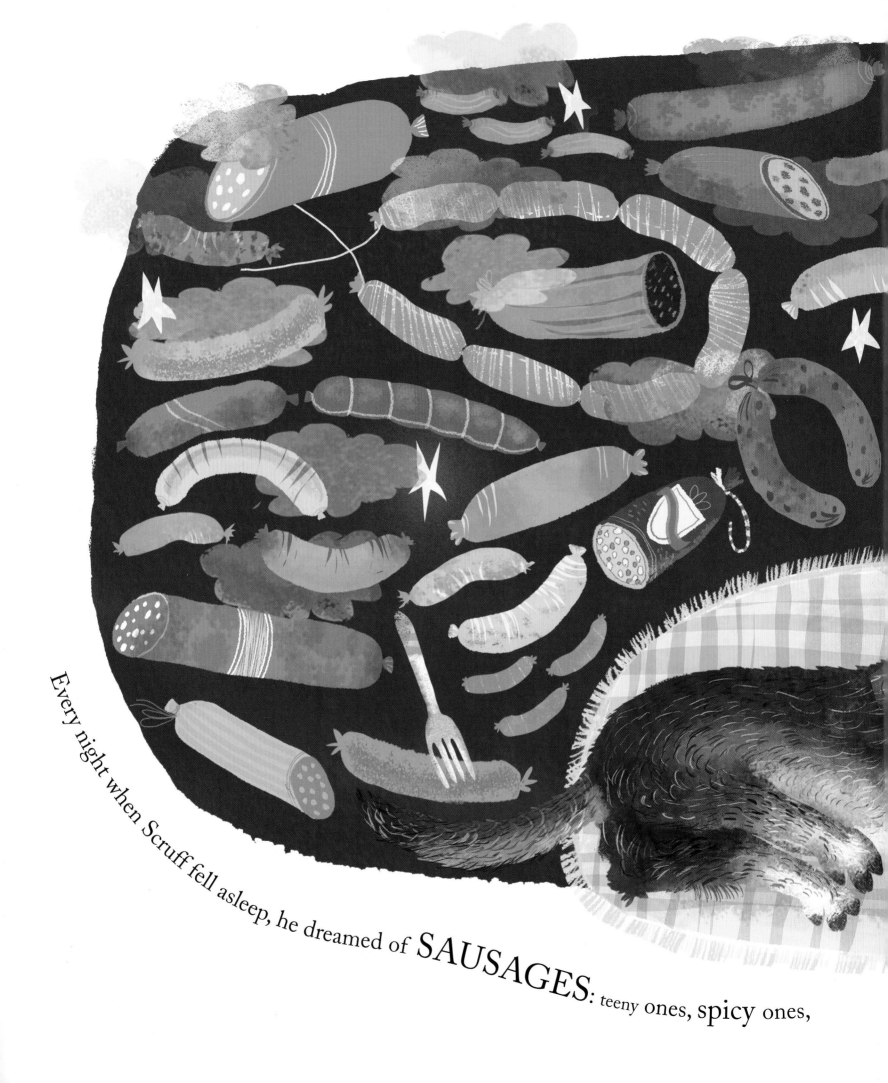

Every night when Scruff fell asleep, he dreamed of SAUSAGES: teeny ones, spicy ones,

big fat juicy ones, curly ones, stinky ones, and even veggie ones!

One fine morning as Scruff stopped for his daily
sniff at the butcher's: SHOCK! HORROR!
Every single sausage had been STOLEN!

THE SAUCY SAUSAGE

...DO NOT CROSS...

...CRIME SCENE - DO NOT CROSS...

100 SAUSAGES STOLEN!

The police chief and the butcher and the mayor held an emergency meeting.
They had their eye on one prime suspect.

The very next day, there were WANTED posters all over town.

"Woof! Double, triple woof!" barked Scruff.

"I must sniff out the **real** culprit before I get put **behind bars!**"

WANTED
FOR SAUSAGE STEALING

HAVE YOU SEEN
THIS DOG?

WANTED
FOR SAUSAGE STEALING

HAVE YOU SEEN
THIS DOG?

Scruff called out to his friends, "Everyone—HELP!
There's a thief on the loose. We need to catch him!"
"I only know how to catch sticks," whimpered Ada the Afghan.

"I can barely catch my breath . . ." huffed Percy the pug.

"I only ever catch colds!" yapped Pixie the poodle.

"I can't even catch my own tail!" sighed Sidney the Dachshund.

"Fine! I'll go and find the thief and **all the stolen sausages** on my own, then," said Scruff.

"Did you say SAUSAGES?" barked Scruff's friends excitedly. And soon they were all trying to think up plans to catch the criminal.

Scruff's plan had three very important steps:

Percy thought he might charm the thief with his dashing good looks!

Ada had always fancied herself as a bit of a detective.

Sidney suggested luring the thief with a cunning disguise.

Pixie was too busy filing her nails to think.

Scruff was about to give up when he detected some **delicious** smells.

STATION

MUSTARD

WANTED
FOR SAUSAGE STEALING

HAVE YOU SEEN
THIS DOG?

HOT DOG
WRAPPER

Led by Scruff, they all marched into town.
There were no signs of the sausage thief anywhere, but there
were plenty of SMELLY clues to investigate.

At last Scruff caught the whiff of simply scrumptious sausages!
As the smell got stronger and stronger, Scruff began to dig

and dig and dig (digging was what Scruff did best). He dug under the wall and came out the other side, where right before his eyes was . . .

the sausage-stealing culprit! Just as Vinnie's van
was zooming off to the market, Scruff managed to
grab a string of stolen SAUSAGES!

He clung on for dear life as the van tried to speed off. Then SMASH! CRUNCH!

It got stuck in a most inconvenient ditch and Scruff's friends leapt aboard to help capture the thief.

The sausage thief was nabbed at last. Everyone cheered, yapped, and barked as Vinnie was carted off to the local police station instead of the local market.

The next day, a very proud mayor, a very grateful butcher,
and a very impressed police chief presented Scruff with a special award:

a big gold ribbon for the best crime-solving,
sausage-sniffing, hole-digging dog in town!

To celebrate, Scruff and his four-legged friends
were treated to a meal at the town's top restaurant.

Can you guess what was on the menu?
Scrumptious, **succulent**, sizzling SAUSAGES!

Scruff was just about to get started on second helpings when . . .

he discovered that Vinnie wasn't the only sausage-stealer in town!

And as for Vinnie, he had to pay
a hefty fine and spend his Saturdays
stuffing sausages—teeny ones, spicy ones,
big fat juicy ones, curly ones, stinky ones,
and even veggie ones!

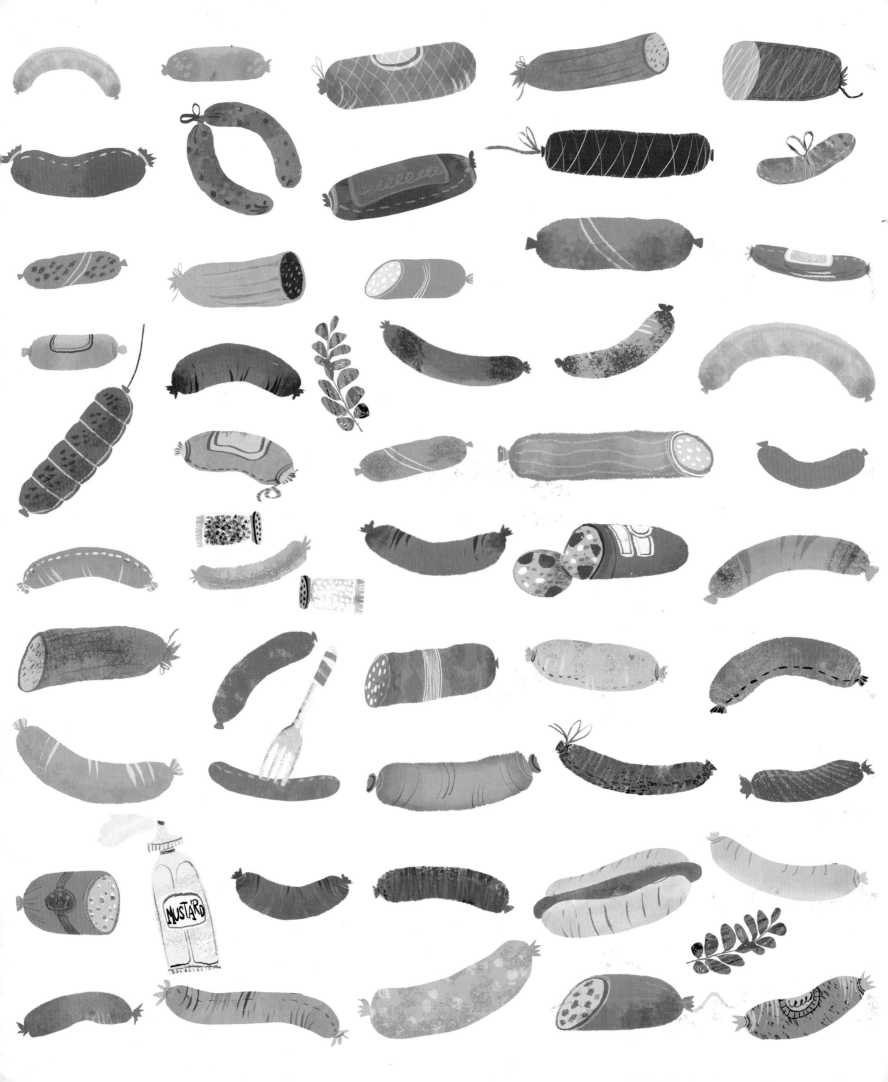